This CHANGE IS STRANGE™ book
was personally made for

With love from

Change Is Strange
And Sometimes scary,
But everyone goes through it.

Jump right in

And give your best.
This book will help you do it.

To Charley
I knew you could do it.

all My Love,

MoMMy

CHANGE IS STRANGE™

Copyright © 2006 by Ricki Booker

No More Pacifier

Part of the CHANGE IS STRANGE™ series

Written by Penny Asher and Ricki Booker
Illustrated by Selena Kassab
Child Development Specialist: Betsy Brown Braun

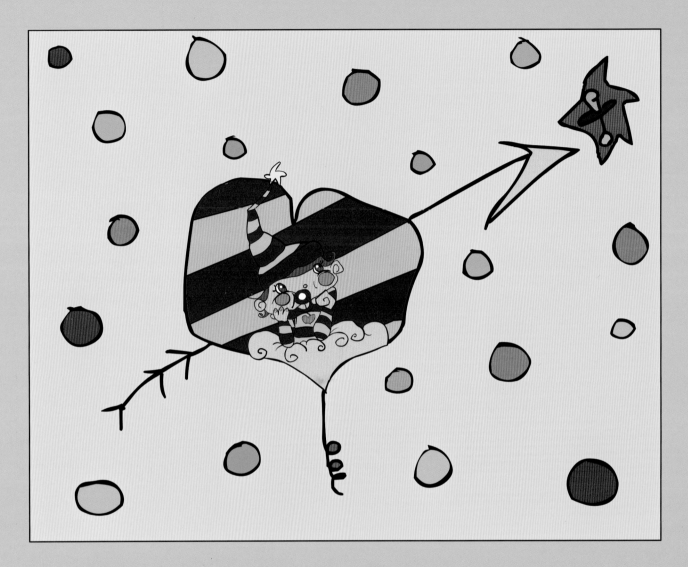

Charlie loved his pacifier. He called it his Binky, and it
was very special to him.

The Binky made Charlie feel warm and snuggly. It reminded him of home.

It calmed him down when he felt sad or angry. Charlie used his Binky all the time.

Sometimes it fell on the ground and got dirty. Sometimes Charlie and Mommy lost it.

Mommy did not love the Binky at all.

Most of all, Mommy worried that the Binky was not good for Charlie's teeth.

"Please take the Binky out," Mommy asked Charlie one day. "I can't understand what you are saying with the Binky in your mouth."

"Please take your Binky out and eat your dinner," Daddy asked one night. "You can't chew with the Binky and food in your mouth at the same time."

"You are too big for the Binky," Mommy said.

Something had to change. It was time for Charlie to give up his Binky.

"I have an idea," said Mommy. "Let's try to use your Binky only at bedtime. We can make a very special box for your very special Binky.

When the sun comes up, you can put your Binky in the box. When it's time for bed, you can take your Binky out of the box. Then, maybe one night you won't need to use the Binky at all."

Charlie didn't want to give up his Binky. *That would be a big change,* Charlie thought. But he decided to give it a try.

Mommy and Charlie found a box that was just the right size. First, they painted the box partly blue. Blue was Charlie's favorite color.

Next, they cut out special pictures and glued them to the box.

When the box was finished, Charlie found a special spot on his shelf and carefully placed his Binky inside the box.

"Remember," Mommy said, "whenever you wake up, put the Binky in the box. When it's bedtime, you can take it out again."

"O.K.," said Charlie. "That sounds like a good plan. I can do that."

Mommy gave Charlie a big hug. "That's my big boy," she said smiling.

Sometimes Charlie thought about his Binky a lot. He wanted it during the day. He wanted it when he felt tired or sad.

I'm not sure I'm ready for this change, thought Charlie.

But every day, putting the Binky in the box got easier

and easier   and easier.

Soon Charlie could play with the other children at the park and not think of the Binky. He could build make believe castles in his bedroom and not think of the Binky. He could go all day long and not think of the Binky.

One night Charlie was very tired. After Mommy read him a bedtime story, Charlie looked at his Binky box on the shelf. He was too sleepy to reach up and get it.

Maybe I don't need my Binky tonight, he thought. *Maybe I can try to go to sleep without it.*

And he did!

When Charlie woke up the next morning, he couldn't wait to tell Mommy and Daddy. The Binky was still in the box on the shelf, right where he had left it.

"I didn't need my Binky last night," Charlie announced.

"That's terrific!" Mommy shouted.

"I am so proud of you!" said Daddy. "You are really growing up."

To celebrate, Mommy and Daddy took Charlie out for a special Pizza Party. "I can talk so much better without my Binky," said Charlie. "You sure can," said Mommy. "I can chew my pizza better without my Binky," said Charlie. "You sure can", said Daddy.

That night Charlie looked at his special Binky box and whispered, "I love you, Binky, but I don't need you anymore. I'm a big boy now."

Maybe he was very, very tired, but he thought he heard the Binky whisper back "That's O.K, Charlie, I understand".

He took the Binky box off his shelf and slipped it in his drawer.

I think I'm going to like this change,
thought Charlie and drifted off to happy dreams.

Helpful Hints For Separating From the Pacifier

1. Read <u>No</u> <u>More</u> <u>Pacifier</u> to your child. Introduce the idea of separating from the pacifier. Ask him/her if he/she is ready to make a *Binky* box.

2. Cut the tip off the end of the pacifier nipple. The child won't get the full effect of sucking and may lose interest.

3. Try inventing the *Binky Fairy*. Let your child know that the *Binky Fairy* is going to visit and take the pacifier and replace it with something else (i.e. a stuffed animal). Talk about the visit in a positive way and let him/her get used to the idea before making the switch.

4. Identify a particular event or thing your child may enjoy and tell him/her that they will have to "buy" it with pacifiers. If your child asks for the pacifiers back, explain that they have already spent them and that they are gone.

5. If there is a new baby on the way, in the family or in the neighborhood, suggest your child is grown up enough to pass the pacifiers on to the baby. This will give your child a sense of pride in being the "big kid", and give the pacifier a home.

WWW.changeisstrange.COM

Come Visit us at
www.changeisstrange.com
to browse other
personalized books
in this series

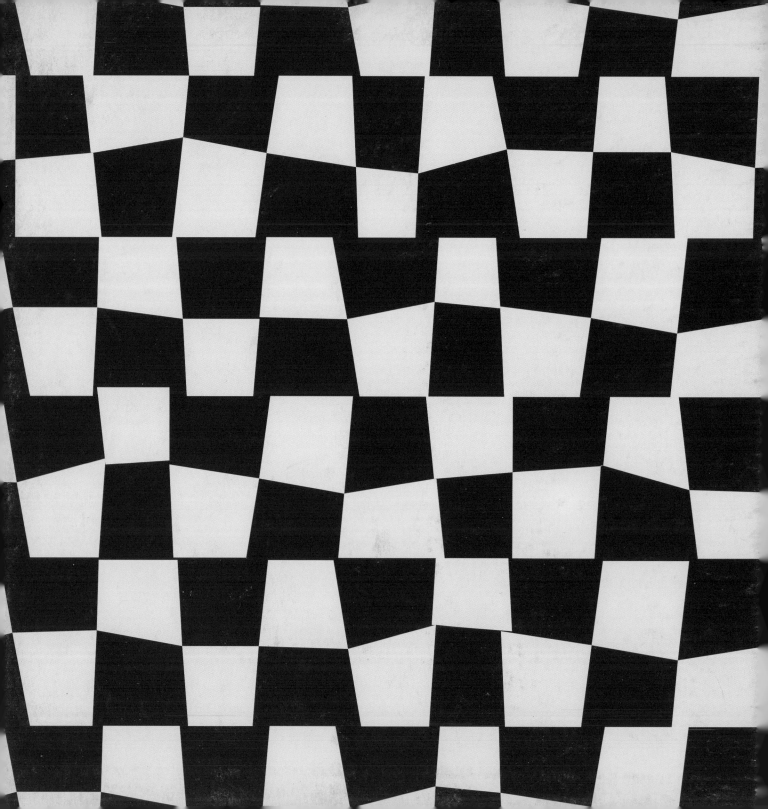